Future Shop

To Kay

Published by Gideon Burrows t/a ngo.media,
75 Gurney Road, Stratford, E15 1SL

ALSO BY GIDEON BURROWS

Fiction

Non-fiction

FUTURE SHOP

GIDEON BURROWS

1

It was like someone had stuck a needle into Rosa's brain from the right hand side, creating a searing headache there above her ear. Her temple was throbbing. Closing her eyes tightly made it go away.

Temporarily.

"Are you ready to proceed, Mrs Bodran?"

Rosa looked up from the fugue to see a good looking man in a suit, with a the latest table technology, called a *slate*, in his hands.

"Yes, yes," said Rosa. "Sorry, had a manic morning. Where were we?"

"I understand, Mrs Bodran. You are a very busy woman. I hope we will help with that today.

"According to the form you filled in, you have three children, at two different schools. You do lots of shopping for the entire family. You like to go on driving holidays in the UK and France. Further than that, you prefer to fly?"

"For my sins," she said.

"We all have choices to make, Mrs Bodran," said the man.

"Call me Rosa, please." His over politeness was doing nothing to ease her headache. Or the slight stomach ache she had.

"Of course. If you are ready, we shall go and see what we have for you, Rosa."

Kieran. That's what it said on his name badge, though she didn't remember him introducing himself. Not with this damn headache. He opened the door and allowed her out into the cold and drizzle.

"The weather is not very friendly," he said. "So unpredictable. Good for you, that you have chosen to test drive our new Urban Tiger. I think you'll find it exactly meets your needs. It gives you the best of both worlds: the busy family life run-around, and the best of comfort and space for those longer drives and holidays."

He sounded like a walking advert.

"It looks great," said Rosa. She eyed the car they were approaching. It was a plum crimson, and she just gasped at her favourite colour, exactly pinned down.

Kieran walked around the vehicle, seemingly ambivalent about the rain. "Our database picked this vehicle out as the best option for you. A big car, easily able to take your family. A large space here at the back, for storing all your shopping. But also, space for your family's luggage during those driving holidays. Rugged on rough ground. But smooth on the road. What do you think?"

"I'd like to give it a test drive," said Rosa, looking up at the worsening rain. She tried to give a meaningful look to the man. Open the damn car.

"It's relatively low emissions, for the brief trips, to schools and back, and it has a super efficient cruise control engine for those longer drives and holidays abroad.

"Oh," and his face suddenly lit up with a smile, "with

this kind of weather, you'll find this vehicle purrs. You will hardly notice the wind, rain and hail. The weather can throw anything at you."

Rosa wondered if Kieran spoke English as a second language. His conversation seemed a little stilted, the phrasing and intonations not quite right.

"Wow," said Rosa, getting wet from the rain. "It might just be the perfect car for us right now, what with the twins."

"Oh, twins. Congratulations. How old are they?"

For a moment, Rosa forgot about the rain. She loved to talk about the kids.

"The two girls are both four. They have an older brother to look after them, he's six."

Kieran just smiled. Rain ran down his face.

"A lot of work. Very time consuming," said Rosa. "In fact..."

"Yes, I understand. Like you said, you're very busy. Well, here is the key fob. Just go ahead, do what you would normally do, and drop it back with me when you have finished. Please enjoy, Rosa."

He gave her a keyring with a crimson square block attached. He turned away, and the rain came down a little heavier.

"Sorry, Kieran?" she called after him, as he slowly walked back to the shelter of his office.

"Rosa?"

"Sorry, am I being dumb? Where are the keys?"

The man turned and walked again in the rain towards her.

"It's an automatic unlock. You are close enough to the car for it to unlock itself. When you walk away, it will lock again. Think of all that shopping. That will be very convenient."

Rosa was embarrassed.

"Very convenient," she said. He gave her a wave and turned again.

Rosa sat in the Tiger's cab, a little pleased to be out of Kieran's company. Maybe he was just the typical creepy salesperson, attempting to slip in the benefits of the car at every opportunity.

She looked at the electronic clock on the dashboard. She had two hours to give the car a decent test drive. She hoped to get the shopping she needed, get the car back to the dealership, then go pick up the kids from school.

There wouldn't be time to see everything the car could do. But Kieran had said she should test drive it as if it were her normal life. To check that it met what she needed, not what she desired. To be honest, he'd already got her at the crimson paintwork. Everything else was going to be secondary.

Climbing into the driver's seat, she'd taken the opportunity to look over towards the back end of the car. The second row was very spacious, plenty for each of the twin's car seats (with suitable safety fixings too) and for Matthew's booster cushion. Seatbelts, naturally.

On the back of her own and the passenger seat were two mini screens, and a little pocket each side with a game controller in.

Only for the longer rides, she promised herself.

Behind the rear row of seats was a huge storage space, enough to take Matthew's bike, if she could ever get him interested in it. Then with plenty of room to spare for camping gear, even one of those mobile fridges. Or else, plenty of shopping space.

There were various hooks and ledges and belts and pockets in the back space, each of which Rosa imagined had been perfectly designed for something or other she would need in the future. She couldn't wait to find out.

Turning back to the dashboard, she liked what it offered. A built in GPS screen and radio. A decent sized glove compartment. A space for takeaway cups. An array of buttons, only some of which she understood. Most of which she didn't.

On the passenger seat was a user manual, which she flicked through to see what the various unfamiliar buttons did.

She could *warm* the automatically adjustable seats. There was an onboard water heater for tea and coffee, presumably powered by the engine. An auto fit button which, when she pressed it, shifted the seat's angle and distance from steering wheel and pedals, exactly to accommodate her height and reach. The mirrors auto tracked too, using her new position to adjust themselves. Now, that was impressive. Particularly if her partner, Sam, was going to be driving the car too.

Finally, she found an 'idling' button. It was for when she needed to park up for a while, but it was wet or freezing outside. And lately, you could never predict when the weather would change. The car would keep her warm, but the fumes from the running engine, which might normally be pushed out into the school carpark, would be temporarily stored. Only to be released when the car was in a more open space.

The brochure also had a section on electric power for this vehicle, but she'd opted out of test driving that model.

At the dealership, she'd felt she had to explain to Kieran that she wasn't confident there were enough charging stations across the UK, and certainly not across the continent. She didn't want to risk being stranded with the kids if the battery went low and there was nowhere to charge.

He didn't seem bothered either way. In fact, he was entirely ambivalent.

"We are here to meet your needs. It is entirely your choice." His favourite phrase of the morning.

Rosa flicked a lever she knew only too well. Windscreen wipers. The front and rear wipers began, and she wondered only for a moment how to adjust their speed. Of course, they were sensitive to the rainfall. She was pleased with how effective they were at keeping the rain from her view.

She checked the time again. She'd already wasted ten minutes admiring the ride. Only one thing more to do. She grabbed the key fob in her hand and looked around.

No key. No hole for a key.

Naturally.

She found a button, surrounded by a glowing circle of green light.

Ignition, it said.

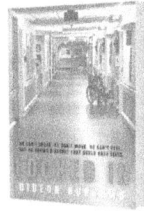   

2

The Urban Tiger did indeed purr into life. Rosa was impressed, but not quite confident enough to use the auto reverse feature that appeared on the dashboard screen.

It seemed to promise her a perfect and safe reverse out of the spot where Kieran had parked the car this morning. But she felt she wanted to use her mirrors. She pushed the car into reverse gear and awkwardly looked over her shoulder. She stretched to see over the raised bonnet and used the mirrors to see all around the vehicle.

She released the hand break and eased her foot back on the brake. The car pulled out and around smoothly, and within 20 seconds she was out of the parking space. Another minute later, she was out of the dealership. The Tiger was already a dream to drive compared to her smaller Corsa, despite its height and bulk.

She hadn't meant to book the test drive for today, but the offer had fitted perfectly with her planned day. It was half day at school, and the advert promised her a free half day of a car most suited to her needs. No obligation to buy and the full use of the vehicle for whatever she wanted.

The dealership was within five miles of school, so she'd been able to drive, drop off the twins, then Matthew, then go straight to meet Kieran.

Now, she was on her way to the shopping trip she'd already planned and marked in her Google calendar for the day.

She aimed to do her usual Monday morning shop. It was something she had down to the minute, in time and efficiency. She would visit Mancro, the large supermarket close to her home. There, she would pick up most of the weekly shop. Cereals, domestic stuff, shampoo, oven ready chips and noodles. The stuff that got the kids fed and made life a little less rushed.

Then she'd head for Frances Road, a cute little High Street that had recently undergone a resurgence. The fried chicken shops had been replaced by artisan bakeries and cafés; mobile phone case shops by a guy who sold fresh fruit, veg and organic flour, and, if you happened to have the empty vessels with you, all manner of oils, coffee grinds and fruit and nut selections.

Next to it, a new shop had taken over from a betting office. It was a Sikh sweet shop, full of sticky colourful balls, made from rice, flours and spices. Rosa loved to sit with one of the sweet balls, taking a coffee and watching the world go by.

Mancro for convenience. The High Street for pleasure. And to support the local community. Low impact, good for the environment and all that. If it had been a normal day, that would be the routine she'd be on just now.

But the test drive was too good an offer to pass up. If she could find a closer Mancro, she *might* still have time for Frances Road.

She hoped the weather wouldn't get any worse. Coffee

and Sikh sweets would be no fun in the rain. And however cute, ambling down the High Street in the soaking wet would be no fun at all.

At the traffic lights, self-consciously though no one else was around, Rosa called out: "Tiger!"

"Yes, Rosa," a voice emerged from the dashboard, as well as in the speakers around her head. "What can I do for you?"

"Nearest Mancro supermarket," she said, very pleased that she was alone.

"Thank you Rosa. The nearest Mancro is at Roding Retail Park. Would you like to go there?"

The voice was almost pitch perfect, with only the slightest nudge of artificial intelligence. It actually sounded like Kieran. She knew these things were programmable. Maybe the chap had selected the closest voice to his own, as part of 'continuing the conversation'. Then she'd buy the car, and he'd earn a big fat commission.

Roding. That was her nearest Mancro, the one she usually went to. And perhaps a little too far. She didn't reply.

"Would you like to consider any alternatives?"

"Okay, yes," said Rosa.

"There is an Avalon Supermarket in 1.3 miles, on Circular Road, Western Embankment. Would you like to go there?"

Rosa hadn't been into an Avalon for an age. Since the kids came along, at least. It was one of those shops that made you feel you were invading people's space if you brought in a child. Lots of old ladies tut-tutting over higher end baking ingredients, or else right up in your baby's face, preventing you from just getting on with the damn shopping.

Maybe it's changed. If not, she didn't have the kids with

her, so she could still get a quick shop done. Perhaps with time left to get to Frances Road.

"Yes, Avalon Supermarket please," she said.

"My pleasure," said Tiger. "Take the next left, in 100 metres."

Rosa felt a little uncomfortable walking away from the Tiger, without physically locking it. Though when she'd gone about ten metres, she heard the car beep and felt the key fob in her hand vibrate.

The rain had set in now, and she welcomed the idea of a shopping centre where she'd be able to get what she needed undercover. If she had the time, she'd still go to the High Street. She could park outside the veg shop and pop to the bakery next door. She might have to miss the coffee and sweets.

At first, Rosa was a little puzzled. There didn't seem to be any trolleys. Usually, she'd have to wrestle one or two rusted ones from each other, try them out for squeaking wheels or biases to one side, to choose one for her shop.

They must be inside.

Avalon was no longer a single supermarket. It had been turned into a mini shopping centre. And to Rosa's surprise, it was full of her favourite stores.

When she walked through the automatic doors, to her right she saw Hawson, the upmarket clothes store she liked to get clothes for herself for a treat, and to dress the kids up nice for parties. Next to that was Lurton Passage, the lovely trinket, sewing and stationery shop. Directly opposite, was Love Baking, the household and baking goods shop and next door, the sports and casual wear shop Freakout. She normally bought their clothes online. She didn't even know they had retail shops.

There was a travel agency next door to that, advertising cheap holidays to Valencia, her favourite Spanish city, in a glass panel at the entranceway. And finally, next to that, a Rescue Children charity shop. She'd always preferred to give to Rescue Children than any other charity. They'd convinced her, in her monthly email, the money was spent directly where it was most needed, home and abroad, to help the neediest kids.

Rosa shook her head. She'd definitely be coming to Avalon again, for a bit of me time. It didn't beat Frances Road, but it was a pretty good wet weather alternative.

She could have gone into any of those stores right now, but she steeled herself away from the branding. She looked right ahead towards the Avalon Supermarket.

Time was ticking.

3

"**M**rs Bodran?"

A sweet looking teenager, not unlike how her son might be in ten years' time, addressed her on the way into the supermarket.

"Sorry, do I know you?"

"No, it's your key fob. Sorry, didn't mean to surprise you. We get the basic data from your car so we can best meet your needs today. I'm Stuart. I don't believe you've been to an Avalon Supermarket before."

Rosa smiled. "Incredible what you can do with technology these days. No, I don't think I've been to Avalon since, well maybe I was a teenager."

"Well, you're very welcome here. We love to show new customers how we work here. Do you have a few minutes, before we get started with your shopping?"

"I'm in a bit of a rush really," said Rosa. "I'd rather just get it done. Where can I get a trolley?"

"Okay, that's fantastic Rosa. If you're short of time, we'll just get the basics done. Would you like to follow me?"

She followed the smart young man, who was dressed in

an Avalon branded polo shirt, as he turned and walked towards some booths. "Take a seat and we'll get you hooked up."

"I'm sorry?"

"The Avalon Shopping Experience is Virtual Reality, Mrs Bodran. I can tell you are on a tight schedule, so this is by far the quickest way to get your shop done. Please, take a seat."

"I'm not sure I'm comfortable with this."

"Mrs Bodran, we have some lovely mints just here. They're designed to deal with any anxiety you might have about trying our latest headset."

She looked at a pair of goggles hung at the side of the comfortable chair she'd just sat down in. They weren't much different from the ones Matthew had for his football game at home. She'd tried to play with him, but losing badly at football had bothered her more than the goggles.

Rosa took one of the mints. It was quite strong, and immediately she found herself concentrating on the taste, rather than nervousness about the VR experience.

Stuart lifted the headset and passed it to Rosa. It felt light in her hands.

"Okay, I'll give it a shot," said Rosa. "But you promise it'll be quicker than just going round the shop myself?"

"Mrs Bodran, or may I call you Rosa, I guarantee it. In fact, I may be able to make it even quicker than your usual shop, if you're able to tell me where you usually go?

"Mancro," she said. "They're pretty good actually, particularly with their scan and shop. You just scan the goods and put them in your bag, ready to go."

"Ah, you must be a member of the Mancro club then? If you give me permission, if you have your club card, I can make you two guarantees: first, you'll do your shopping quicker than you do at Mancro; and second, I guarantee you'll get your usual shop cheaper."

"You're quite the salesperson," said Rosa, smiling. "Are you sure you're not going to harvest my mind?"

He laughed out loud. "No more than clicking on one of those pop-up cookie requests on the web does."

Rosa smiled. She fished her phone from her handbag and brought up the Mancro app. She held it up for Stuart to take.

"That's okay," he said. "Just look at your phone screen with the headset. Then we can get started."

"Hah, what's the downside?" said Rosa.

"Well, that's for you to tell us. Avalon is always on the lookout for feedback. Positive or negative. Ready to go? It is entirely your choice."

Rosa pulled on the VR headset. She found it fitted well and wasn't so heavy it forced her head down.

"I'm sure you'll find them very comfortable, once you get used to them," said Stuart.

Rosa looked around. It was as if she was wearing sunglasses. She could still see Stuart and her booth, only there was a slight tint to the screen.

"Okay," she said. "How do we get started?"

Her goggles brightened.

Empty shelves.

Rosa was standing in an aisle of Avalon Supermarket, wearing the headset, but all she could see were empty shelves and Avalon branding.

She looked around her, behind, up, and down. There

was nothing but empty shelves. No other customers, no staff, and no Stuart.

"Hello?" she called out.

"Hello, Rosa," Stuart said. He was standing in front of her and the trolley she now had. She must have missed him.

"Can you look at your Mancro card for me?" he said. "The barcode?"

Rosa looked down at her phone and it beeped as the goggles centred on the square Quick Code image.

"That's excellent, Rosa," said Stuart. "Enjoy your shop. I'll be right here."

When Rosa looked up from the card, she watched as the shelves on the aisle in front of her appeared to be filling. Closer to her, they were already packed. Towards the end of the aisle, products were slowly emerging and placing themselves on shelves.

"Wow," she said.

She looked around her. Immediately to her right were stacks of baked beans, ready to cook tortellini pasta, ready made pizzas, frozen sausages. On the shelf below it, were blocks of cheese (strength 4), tubs of margarine, milk (two litre bottles of semi skimmed, one litre bottles of skimmed), natural Greek yoghurt (1/2 litre), and packages of a dozen tiny fruit yoghurts. There were veggie burgers and sausages, washing tabs, dishwasher tabs, school lunch bars.

Rosa shook her head. Exactly her usual shopping items, right here in front of her. If this was how it was going to go, Stuart was dead right about it being a quicker shop. Some brands weren't the same, but most were.

She reached out for a box of fruit and fibre cereal, but was startled when her hand appeared to move through it. She quickly drew her hand back, half scared, half puzzled.

"Just take it more gently," Stuart said. "The system is very sensitive."

Rosa reached to the shelf again, and more deftly this time, picked up the box of cereal. It was lighter in her hand than she expected.

"We're still working on the weight of things," said Stuart from behind her. "But we're getting there. Go ahead, put it in your trolley."

As if cradling a bird, Rosa moved the box across from the shelf and lowered it into the trolley. She gently released it only when she felt it rest on the bottom.

"You'll get used to it," said Stuart. "Try again."

"It feels funny," she said.

"We hope it will feel like fun," he said. "Then become second nature."

Rosa reached out, this time for a two litre bottle of milk. She expected it to be cold to the touch, but it felt just the same as the weight and temperature of the cereal.

"Oh, that feels weird," she said.

"Like I say, we're working on the exact experience. We're getting closer every day. But we have hundreds of thousands of products."

Rosa put the milk in her trolley, a little more confident now.

"Go on, reach for one more of your goods," Stuart said.

This time, Rosa went for a big bag of pasta, fusilli wholemeal, the stuff the three kids would eat up in piles, if sprinkled with cheese.

She dropped it into the trolley.

An almost transparent blue square screen appeared in front of Rosa, floating above her trolley.

Stuart said out loud what was written there, in the Avalon font and branding colours.

"Hey, it looks like you're doing your usual family shop. Would you like to add everything you usually buy to your trolley? Swipe right for yes, and left for no. And remember, you can remove and replace items in your trolley at any time. It's entirely your choice."

"Okay, wow. I'm liking this," said Rosa.

She swiped her hand in front of the screen, to the right. In dramatic fashion, the produce from all around her, and right down the aisle before her, appeared to leave their shelves. In an arc, they moved through the air and landed gently into her trolley.

Surely there were more goods than could fit in, but they seemed to slot themselves neatly into the space she had.

She gasped again. It was far from the piled-up mess of goods she usually came out of the supermarket with, even after they'd been self-scanned. She would take bags in, intending always to get certain products in certain bags - crisps, crackers, breads together here; cold stuff like milk, cheese and butter there; washing up, clothes cleaning, shoe polish there - but by the end of a shop, she'd just be piling on top, promising she'd sort it neatly when she got to the car. She never did. She just flung it into the back, and would try to persuade a grumpy Matthew to bring some stuff in when she got home.

Now, all of her goods were in neat order. She noticed most of the goods went together in the trolley, in the same way she would put them together in her cupboards. The bread bin. The cereal cupboard. The fridge. The freezer. Even the 'don't quite know where this should go, so I'll put it in here' cupboard.

She smiled again and thought about tea.

No, she couldn't make another curry. It was a favourite of hers and Sams, and an easy win when in a rush. But the kids had said they were bored with it (they were never bored with pasta).

She looked down and noticed a jar of ready made curry sauce. It wasn't her usual brand, but it was the same strength that Sam liked. She gently picked up the jar, which again felt weird in weight. She realised she'd have to walk further up the aisle to put it back where it had come from.

Or, she thought, she could do what most people do. Sneak it back onto the shelf where she was and make a run for it.

She made to do that, a little nervously, even though there were no other shoppers around her. But with the uncertainty of holding the curry sauce jar, its peculiar weight and feel, she dropped it.

She sprang back a little, expecting it to hit the ground, smash and splatter the floor and her shoes with curry. But the jar seemed to hover in the air, before it arced into the distance, and placed itself back on the shelf again.

"Wow, now this could be fun," she said aloud.

She looked around for something else she didn't need. Salt. She always bought too much of it. She picked it up and dropped it out of the trolley. Like the curry sauce, it flew and landed neatly on the shelf.

She looked at her watch. She'd been shopping for five minutes maximum and had already completed most of it.

She was enjoying herself more than she'd ever done at Mancro. At this rate, she'd have loads of time to spend in Freakout and maybe even catch a look at that Valencia offer.

"Right," she said aloud. "What's next?"

4

Rosa quickly got the hang of the Avalon Shopping Experience. From her 'favourites' aisle, she turned a corner and saw before her a series of Avalon branded signs hanging from the ceiling.

Ready meals

Rice & pasta

Household cleaning

Frozen

Snacks

Alcohol

When she caught herself, she smiled. She barely noticed that she was actually sitting in a chair, in a private booth, doing all her shopping through a VR headset.

It all felt so real.

And instead of wading through the aisles she never went through - dog food, cat litter, baby goods (though she had a strange feeling of nostalgia for that aisle) - to get to those she did, the aisles she most often visited were already closest to her.

Of course, if she wanted budgie seed, she expected she would be able to find it. But otherwise, she could ignore whole swathes of the supermarket.

The VR experience prioritised her favourite aisles. The ones she most liked to browse, even if she wasn't looking for anything specific.

Like the bread aisle. Everyone likes the bread aisle. The pancakes, crumpets, pittas, then soda farls, sour dough, even focaccia.

She didn't *need* any bread, other than the usual loaf she'd loaded in her Mancro shop. But she wanted to take her usual gentle stroll down that aisle, anyway. She was a bread tourist. She had a fancy for something really salty, anyway. Some crackers, perhaps.

She swiped the sign above her: Breads.

The aisle approached her. Or did she approach the aisle? She imagined she could smell fresh bread cooking. Had Avalon somehow captured that sweet smell, and was pumping it into her booth right now? She wouldn't be surprised.

She sauntered down the aisle, loving the variety, the shapes, the different thicknesses, the roundness, the loaves scattered with seeds, or glowing in the supermarket lights.

She grabbed some Scotch pancakes, a treat for the kids, and some salty crackers for herself. She'd open those as soon as she got into the car.

At the end, she saw a fresh bakes section: cream cakes, meringues, chocolate cookies, sweetly decorated birthday cakes with footballers, cartoon characters and princesses. Boy did she love the bread aisle.

She decided she probably wouldn't have time to get to the High Street after all. Instead, she would swipe six loose pain au chocolat into her trolley. She was tempted to pick one up, squeeze it, feel its soft crunch. She swore she could smell chocolate.

Oh, if only the VR experience could give her a proper feeling, she'd be in heaven. To hold the bread to her nose, squeeze it and bring in that freshly baked odour. Surely that was on the to do list of the supermarket. And if it was, sign her up.

She looked at each of the freshly made cream cakes and donuts. They appeared to be the real thing. Not pixilated, not like a photograph. And each one, each cream bun or apple turnover, was slightly different. It wasn't one apple turnover copied and pasted, like you might see online.

"Good morning, Mrs Bodran,"

She looked up from the pastries. There was a woman dressed in a chef's uniform behind the counter.

"Oh, hi," Rosa said, feeling like she ought to step back in surprise, but noticing she was still sitting in a chair.

"Looks like you have an eye on those apple turnovers?" the chef said. "They're delicious. Would you like to try a sample?"

"I'm sorry?"

"Would you like to try a sample of the apple turnovers? It's something new we're trialling here at Avalon. Adding a taste element to our VR experience."

"What, you mean I can taste something?"

"Actually, only a few products in this department. But lucky enough for you, those turnovers were a favourite for the taste test."

"Well, it feels weird," said Rosa.

"Of course. And everything here at Avalon is entirely your choice. I understand."

"Do you?"

"I'm sorry, Mrs Bodran, can you repeat that?"

"Do you understand? I mean, are you real?"

"Mrs Bodran, I am part of your Avalon Shopping Experience. I am as real as you need me to be."

"So, you're not really a, well, a baker?"

"My name is Shellie Mason, and I am part of your Avalon Shopping Experience. I'm based on a real baker, who was part of the team that designed this experience. I'm as real as you need me to be."

Rosa felt a little uncomfortable.

"So, you're what, a hologram? And you're offering me the experience of tasting something that doesn't really exist?"

"I'm a Virtual Reality Assistant, offering you a Virtual Reality experience, Mrs Bodran. The end result, should you decide to taste the apple turnover, and indeed buy one, is that you will have a real apple turnover, of the same approximate taste and, we hope, texture, to take home with you."

Just for a moment, Rosa felt the headache in her right temple getting worse. She didn't know whether to taste it.

"Stuart?" she said.

"Hello Rosa, how can I help you?" The young man was standing beside her, as if he'd been there all along.

"I'm not sure I want to carry on. I'm feeling a little weirded out."

"Thanks Rosa, that's really useful to know. As I've said, we're taking on board all feedback. You're giving me the impression that this interaction doesn't feel comfortable for you?"

"It's not the baker," she turned to the woman in the baker's uniform, who just smiled. Rosa turned to a whisper. "It's more like, being asked to do something that is virtual and unusual, by something that is virtual and unusual.

"No offence," she said to the baker. She just smiled back.

"I would like to try the apple turnover, though."

Stuart smiled. "Of course, Rosa. No to the baker, yes to the offer to try the apple turnover."

"I guess?"

"Would you like me to switch off all VR human interaction at this position today?"

"There's more?" asked Rosa.

"At the meat counter, the fish counter and we also have a public demonstration area. We're trying to realistify the most common human interactions first. To test them, just like right now with Shelley."

"At least you're not realisifying other shoppers," said Rosa, pleased with herself. "They're the worst. Getting in the way, shoving you out of the way to get to the eggs first."

Stuart didn't smile.

"Mrs Bodran, our research suggested that many people's shopping experiences would be vastly improved without other shoppers. We have already identified that it is your preference. But if you would like to try…"

"No, thank you. It's hard enough shopping with the kids."

Stuart smiled. Rosa looked towards the cakes again. The baker had disappeared.

"I have turned off the baker experience. So, Mrs Bodran, would you like to try some of this apple turnover?"

Rosa hesitated. If she was going to make the most of this VR experience, she ought to give it a go. She needn't come back if she didn't enjoy it.

"Okay, yes."

"Go ahead then," said Stuart. "Take a piece."

Rosa hadn't noticed there was a plate of apple turnover on the top of the counter, sliced into neat parts, each with a wooden stick poked through the middle.

She raised her eyebrows.

"So, I just take it?"

"Yes, Mrs Bodran, help yourself. It's entirely your choice."

Rosa took a piece of turnover from the plate. This time, she felt some weight to it, and as she moved it towards her mouth, she caught the distinct smell of caramelised brown sugar and the acidity of sugared apples.

She shook her head. She couldn't believe she was doing it.

She put it into her mouth, and immediately tasted the apple and caramel, followed by butter in the pastry.

"Oh, wow, that's weird," she said, instinctively moving her hand up to cover her mouth, as if she didn't want to speak with her mouth full.

But there was no sensation of something actually in her mouth, only the taste.

"It's delicious. I mean, superb. And really realistic," she said.

"That's fantastic, Mrs Bodran."

Rosa swallowed, but the taste lingered for a few moments more. Then, abruptly, it went away.

"Oh, it's gone," Rosa said.

"Yes, it's all a work in progress," said Stuart. "Different people naturally taste things for different times. Some swallow before others. Some want the actual feel of the food in their mouths, some don't. But we're working on it."

"You can't please everyone all the time?"

"We're working on it," said Stuart.

"Okay, I'm convinced about the apple turnovers at least." She swiped five from the counter. A treat for the kids, and something to share with Sam when they got home.

She had only the slightest awareness that she'd unintentionally bought pancakes, pain au chocolat and now apple turnovers. Far more than she'd come in for.

5

Rosa tried to switch her mind off temptation and browsing, and instead to what she knew the family actually needed. Aside from her usual shop.

Some extra dishwasher tablets, and some freshener for the tumble drier.

She reached up and swiped the Household sign. In moments, she was at the end of the aisle, and before her on the first shelf was the brand of dishwasher and fresheners she usually bought. Behind them were other options.

She swiped what she wanted into her basket.

A blue square appeared above her trolley, along with Stuart's voice.

"Choose another product from this aisle and get it for half price."

Rosa's heart began to beat. She didn't strictly need anything else on display, but half price was too good to turn down. More fabric conditioner? Dishwasher salt? Rinse aid? She had loads at home already, but it could just be put under the sink.

Fabric conditioner was the most expensive, so she

figured, by taking another bottle, she had the most to gain. She swiped it into her basket.

She then went to the tea and coffee aisle. Again, she was presented with the brands she'd usually take: ready roasted coffee beans for her own grinder. A ground decaffeinated. Then the normal tea brand she'd take in bags. Plus boxes of herbal tea: green tea, camomile, mixed berry. Behind it were teas she rarely bought, but had in the past.

She knew some coffee had already gone into the trolley because it was her usual shop, but she opted for a bag of decaf ready ground.

Again, a blue square sign appeared before her:

"The brand you have chosen is not approved by the Rainforest Foundation. At Avalon, we work closely with our suppliers to provide you with options, and would be pleased to suggest alternatives. It's entirely your choice. Are you happy to continue?"

She'd never considered it before.

Rosa remembered there had been lots of debate about coffee and rainforests years ago. She thought all the companies had come on board with one or another certification standard. She hadn't thought about her coffee choices since then.

She swiped left for no.

"That's great. Let me recommend Avalon's partner brand Derigot Decaffeinated Coffee, 300g, ground coffee. £4.50 per pack, fully certified by the Safe Rainforest Foundation. It is entirely your choice. Are you happy to continue? Or would you like to consider other options?"

Rosa thought. It was £1 more expensive than her usual brand of decaf. But if it was going to save the orang-utans, or whatever, a £1 here and there wouldn't hurt. Then she thought of the car she'd driven in to get to Avalon.

Quickly, she swiped the recommended coffee into her trolley.

"That's great," said Stuart. "We're doing all we can at Avalon to make the world a better place. Would you like us to guide you through other ethical choices in the store?"

She swiped yes on the opaque blue square. After the decaf, she really couldn't say no.

"That's great. Please select which of the following topics most concern you:
- Animal rights
- Climate change
- Species dilapidation
- Human rights
- Economic inequality
- Packaging

She blew out air in a quick huff, as if it was a simple choice between them. She hit 'Human rights'.

"That's great. The rest of your shop will take that preference into account though you can, of course, select any goods you wish from the thousands of items we stock."

That's great, thought Rosa. Except she wished Stuart, or the computer or whatever, would stop saying just how great it was.

"Before we get started," Stuart said, "do you want us to analyse what is already in your shopping trolley and offer to replace products rated higher on our human rights rating list? Remember, it's entirely your choice, and you can add and remove goods."

Rosa swiped left for no. For the rest of the shop, okay, she'd let Avalon recommend. But she didn't want to unload what she'd already placed there. If she started all that, her shopping would take longer.

Then again, there wasn't much left to buy, was there?

Just some meat for tonight's tea with Sam (now curry was off the agenda), and - given the weather - she'd seek something super convenient for the kids. They were bound to come in from school with wet shoes and miserable that they couldn't play outside yet again.

She swiped Ready Meals from the central aisle and immediately saw her kids' favourite: the big ready to cook Italian Feast Bag. It wasn't the same brand as Mancro offered, but the idea was the same. A ready for the oven lasagne for two (easily split over three kids), two garlic breads, pre-buttered and cooked, ready to go in the oven for ten minutes, a bag of salad, a plastic pot of ready to eat pitted olives, and a box of crostini crackers to keep the kids busy while waiting for the lasagne to cook.

She swiped it into her bag.

Next to the ready meals, she found a small shelf of wines she must have missed. Her favourite red Valpolicella, of course. Designed to complement the lasagne ready meal, but would do great for her and Sam with whatever the meat counter had to offer.

She swiped a bottle into the trolley, and the blue screen appeared, with Stuart's voice.

"We have a special for you on Italian wines today. Would you like to add another bottle, at a 10% discount?"

Of course she would. For a supermarket, this Valpolicella was the best. Buying two bottles here at Avalon would cheaper than buying two at Mancro.

It made Rosa salivate. Tonight was going to turn into quite the evening. She imagined the rain heaving down, her and Sam cuddled up inside, sharing an intimate meal once the kids were asleep. A bottle of the Italian red. Perhaps more.

Olive oil, she thought. If we're going to have red, and go

Italian, she should get some olive oil. She could take a focaccia bread. And then Sam and she could have some to dip in oil, just like they had on that last minute book and fly to Milan they did last year.

She looked up at the aisle. Where would the olive oil be?

"Stuart?"

"Hello Rosa, how can I help you?"

"I'm looking for olive oil?"

"It's right here," he said, "in the oil and condiments section."

Rosa looked around, and before her was a stack of various oils, including the brand she normally took.

She went to swipe it into her trolley.

A blue square appeared above her trolley, along with Stuart's voice.

"This brand is made with olives grown in Israel. Our customers have previously expressed concern with the human rights record of that country, and after careful consideration we have thus rated this brand as 50% ethical according to our human rights standard. We do stock olive oil with higher human rights ratings. Would you like to consider them?"

Rosa shook her head. She barely knew anything about the Arab-Israeli conflict, only what she'd heard on the news. She didn't really have a view. And she wasn't sure about the effectiveness of boycotts.

"Okay, let me see the alternatives."

On the shelf before her, three brands - completely new to Rosa - appeared. She picked one up.

"Rancolini olive oil has been rated as 75% ethical on our human rights rating, because of uncertainty in the supply chain and the condition of workers involved in picking."

She picked up another

"Redro olive oil has been rated as 80% ethical on our human rights rating, because of uncertainly in the supply chain and concerns expressed by our customers about the human rights record of Turkey."

"Jesus," said Rosa. She picked up the third.

"Saluda Bien olive oil has been rated as 70% ethical on our human rights rating, because of uncertainty in the supply chain, and concerns expressed by our customers about the condition of workers involved in picking."

Rosa sighed.

"Okay, Stuart, which am I supposed to pick?"

"It is entirely your choice. We aim to provide you with the information you need to make the right choices for you."

"So, do you have any 100% ethical olive oil?" She felt a fool for asking the question. It sounded so lame and so, well, middle class. Ethical olive oil, for God's sake.

"Regarding your option to be notified about human right's based shopping choices, we have now presented you with the most favourable options," said Stuart.

"Okay, scrap the human rights for a moment."

"You want me to switch off your human rights preference?"

"Yes. How does it look now?"

"I'm sorry, Mrs Bodran, can you rephrase the question?"

"Which is the most ethical olive oil you have in stock?"

"Thanks for your question, Mrs Bodran, that's great. Our ethical recommendations are determined by the considerations you feel are most important to you."

The blue square appeared again, above her trolley.

Please select which of the following topics of most concern you:

- Animal rights
- Climate change

- Species dilapidation
- Human rights
- Economic inequality
- Packaging

If she wasn't wearing the VR goggles, Rosa would have smacked her head. She just wanted some bloody olive oil. Her lovely picture of dining with Sam tonight was rapidly diminishing. She hadn't expected a philosophy class.

She looked at the list, crossed her arms, and thought. She tried to second guess: the bottles were plastic, which probably meant packaging was out, climate change too. Human rights were already too tricky. Animal rights? She was about to visit the meat counter, so let's not even go there. Economic inequality could bring up the worker's conditions again.

"I'll go for species dilapidation," she said, while swiping the option.

Silence.

"So, which are the most ethical choices now?" Rosa said.

"None of our olive oils are rated negatively regarding species dilapidation. Remember...

"It is entirely my choice, yes I get it," said Rosa.

"From the thousands of products on sale," Stuart finished.

"Thank God for that," said Rosa. She took her normal brand back off the shelf, though she promised herself she would look up the conflict when she next got a few moments.

6

_____

With olive oil, red wine and the kids' tea in hand, Rosa felt a visit to the meat counter would be enough to finish her shop.

She was aware she was still shopping far more quickly than she usually would, but the brief lectures and extra choices were grating.

She looked up at the signs down the main aisle and selected the Fresh Meat counter. Immediately, she was against the counter, looking at the produce on offer.

To the front, as she was now getting used to, were the meat products she often bought. But not so often she hadn't auto swiped into her trolley earlier.

Despite the stumble over the olive oil, she was still looking for something special for her and Sam.

She purposefully avoided any of the things she normally bought. Time for a surprise for Sam, and something untested by her. She liked the look of some thick curled up sausages behind her usual choices. They looked like they were seasoned with herbs and spices.

"Hello, Mrs Bodran," said the butcher, who seemed to appear from nowhere.

"I am Herbert Fielding. Would you like me to assist you today?"

"Yes, those curled sausages at the back," she said.

"Those are our finest Cumberland sausages. We make them with fresh pork, with white and black pepper, thyme, sage, nutmeg and just a touch of spice. They're a big seller this time of year, barbecue season."

"Mmm, not much chance of a barbecue in this weather?"

"I'm sorry, Mrs Bodran, could you rephrase the question?"

"Oh, no, it doesn't matter. It's just, the rain."

The butcher just stood behind the counter, smiling.

"What about steaks," said Rosa.

"We have our perfect rump steak, also good for the barbecue, or pre-made minced beef burgers that will be great flame grilled."

"I'm sorry," said Rosa. "Have you seen the rain? I don't think we'll be having a barbecue soon."

"I'm very sorry, Mrs Bodran. I thought you were looking for barbecue meat. This weekend, according to your online calendar, you have agreed to go to a barbecue at a friend's house, number 35 Downshire Lane, Milton Keynes, MK18. Would you like me to trace that booking?"

"Oh, yes. This weekend." Rosa shook her head, feeling the goggles shake with her.

"One moment. Yes, I have found a WhatsApp message group, in which the word barbecue and the abbreviation BBQ have been mentioned recently.

"Friends from Uni" - *"looking forward to our annual BBQ, we're hosting this year"*

Mandy; "we're right there at the barbecue on Saturday"

PPPJam; "kids looking forward to Saturday, barbecue, we'll bring a tent"

"Okay, I get it, thank you. Barbecue this Saturday," said Rosa. "Only, I don't think it's going to happen. What with the rain?"

The butcher just stood and smiled.

"Can I recommend our perfect rump steak, good for the barbecue, or pre-made minced beef burgers that will be great flame grilled."

Rosa smiled and shook her head. "No, thank you. Let's go for chicken. Convenience. No barbecue shopping today."

"Of course, it's entirely your choice."

"I think I'll leave the meat, actually."

"Of course," said the butcher. "Here at Avalon, it is entirely your choice, from our thousands of products on sale."

She felt she'd give a punch to the next person, or hologram, or whatever, to say that.

She looked up, and the nearest option to her on the signs above was the fish counter. She swiped it, and was immediately standing behind a wide range of fish and seafood presented on ice.

This time, she felt cold. She wasn't sure if that was from real ice in front of her, something happening in the cubicle she had almost forgotten she was sitting in, or whether her brain had just invented it to match was she was watching.

"Hello, Mrs Bodran," said the woman fishmonger behind the counter. "Would you like me to assist you today?"

"No, thank you, I'm just browsing."

"Of course. Please let me know if I can help with anything. Here at Avalon, it is entirely your choice."

Rosa crossed her arms.

"Cod," she thought. "Cod, plain and simple." She could cook it, maybe even batter it, flash fry it with oil, and she and Sam could have an upmarket fish and chips. She was suddenly convinced this was her greatest idea for ages, and her next designation would be the booze aisle to pick up some real ale. A proper pub tea, only at home.

It wasn't hard to find, but looked pricey. Still, with the real ale in mind, and the potato wedges she now had planned, it would be worth it for a decent night in with Sam.

She swiped two pre-prepared cod into her basket.

A blue square appeared above her trolley, and the voice of Stuart accompanied it.

"The choice you have made is North Sea cod. Our customers have previously expressed concern with regards to low fish stock in UK waters, because of overfishing and disputed fishing rights. Mackerel, haddock, Scottish lobsters and North Sea cod are noted as overfished and facing collapse, according to campaign groups. At Avalon, we have rated North Sea cod as 20% ethical on our species dilapidation index. We do stock other fish and seafood varieties with higher dilapidation index scores. Would you like to consider them?"

"No Stuart," Rosa barked. "I just want some cod."

"Of course, Rosa, it's entirely your choice…"

"And can you turn that bloody ethical choice thing off? I'm fed up of being lectured about my shopping."

"Of course, Rosa, we aim to make the shopping experience convenient and enjoyable for our customers."

The blue square disappeared, and so did Stuart. The fish moved into her trolley, and she felt the cold dissipate as she moved away from the counter.

She looked at her watch. She'd still only been shopping for ten minutes or so. Why did it feel like an hour?

It was certainly quicker. Perhaps, she just needed to get used to it. Stuart had warned about that. But Avalon needed to get used to shopping her way, too. At least this was a trial.

Now, where was that booze?

7

Beautifully presented before her were rows upon rows of her favourite wines and beers. The deep Rioja she'd thought about earlier was on the second shelf. A preferred wine, she thought, but not one she drank often so enough that it was offered to her first at Avalon.

She was getting this.

She swiped two bottles into her trolley. One for tonight, another for the weekend and whatever that turned out to be, now that the barbecue looked like it would move indoors.

She turned, and immediately behind her found shelves of beers. She swiped a six pack of ale into the trolley. She browsed and found a small bottle of sherry. She thought she might make a trifle or some other suitably boozy desert for the weekend party.

A red square appeared above her trolley, with Stuart's voice backing it up.

"Hello, Rosa. We've noticed you've placed several alcoholic beverages in your shopping trolley. We would like to offer you information about healthy alcohol intake, and have a number of support lines we can refer you to. Remember, it's entirely your choice."

"Holy crap, it's just a few bottles. Stuart, what have I bought?"

"2 bottles, 750cl, San Jose Rioja at 17% avb.

2 bottles, 750cl, Merido Red at 13% avb

1 bottle, 750cl, Avalon finest red wine at 16% avb

Six pack of Gurder Ale, 330cl per can, at 5% avb

Six pack of Smiths Brown Ale, 330cl per can, at 4.5% avb

1 bottle, 500cl, Finest Dark Sherry, 17.5% avb."

For a moment, Rosa was puzzled. Had Stuart sneaked in the extra six pack and the Avalon Red? Then she realised, it must have been loaded into her trolley at the beginning when she swiped all of her favourites.

To be honest, it looked like a lot of booze when it was listed like that. But anything extra could sit on the shelf at home, couldn't it?

Five bottles of wine, a bottle of sherry, and eight cans of beer? Who was she kidding?

She and Sam had got into the habit of a tipple every night before bed. The kids could be so stressful, the couple deserved it, didn't they?

"Okay, we'll get rid of one bottle of the Italian white," she said aloud, finding it and dropping it out of her trolley. It flew to a distant shelf on the booze aisle.

The blue screen appeared, with Stuart's voice. "We have a special for you on Italian wines today. Would you like to add another bottle, at a 10% discount?"

She stood in front of a row of bottles of Italian wines, exactly opposite the Valpolicella she'd just dumped.

"Hold on, that's just what I've got rid of? Now you're asking me if I want to pick it up again?"

"Remember, it's entirely your choice, and you can add and remove goods at any time."

"Then I want the wine," she said. She swiped the same wine back into her trolley.

The red square again.

"Hello, Rosa. We've noticed you've placed a number of alcoholic beverages in your shopping trolley. We would like to offer you information about healthy alcohol intake, and have a number of support lines we can refer you to. Remember, it's entirely your choice."

"Yes, it certainly is. Where's your bloody vodka?"

A shelf flew towards her. She picked up the nearest bottle to her, the brand she bought occasionally. She dropped it into her trolley.

If she wasn't test driving that brand new Tiger, she'd thought, she might be tempted to sink a shot of it right now.

Talking of which.

She looked at her watch. If the weather hadn't improved, she would not make it to the High Street, to buy fruit and veg locally, then get the test car back to the dealership before going to pick the kids up from their half day.

She swiped the sign for fresh produce. There, she dashed down the aisles, swiping in the produce she'd normally pick up from the local grocers. She noticed, because she didn't have a track record of buying fresh produce from Mancro, she had to browse the shelves herself. Her favourite goods weren't stacked up, ready for her to simply swipe into the trolley.

On the High Street, she would usually have time to chat with Matt, the friendly young 'veg man', who would drive down to the import markets at 4 a.m. each day, to bring produce fresh off the boat to his shop and his customers by the time he opened at 8 a.m.

He'd only offer what was in season, or freshly imported, and by lunchtime would often have run out of stock. It only proved his determination to keep things fresh.

She thought of him as she swiped her fruit and veg into the trolley. A huge bag of carrots, three broccoli, each individually wrapped. A bag of leeks, a punnet of easy peel oranges, another of grapes. A bag of potatoes. Parsnips, sweet potatoes. Bananas.

By the end, she had a week's worth of veg which added up to a vast quantity. But cost wise, she estimated, it added up to probably a single visit to Matt's shop, where she'd get less than half of what she'd chosen.

"Stuart," she said.

"Hello, Mrs Bodran, how can I help you?"

"How much have I spent?"

He told her, including spelling out the discounts she'd received with buy one get one frees, and special offers.

"We've priced matched your usual shop with Mancro supermarket. And our data suggests you have made a significant saving on your fresh produce against what you would have paid for those goods at Mancro or any of our leading competitors."

Rosa looked at the number on the screen. Still, it was for a week's shopping, done and dusted, and guaranteed to be cheaper.

Time to get out of here before she bought the whole place.

———

Rosa swiped the sign above her that said Payment and quickly found herself in front of a checkout unit.

"Hello, Mrs Bodran, thank you for your visit today," a kind looking woman said.

"Hi."

"We noticed you have the breakfast cereal, Malted Wheats, in your shopping today. We find many of our customers also buy Malt Wheat Flakes with that product. Would you like to add a box to your shopping today?"

"No, thank you," said Rosa.

"We noticed you have the bread product breakfast pancakes in your shopping today. We find many of our customers also buy Avalon pancake syrup with that product. Would you like to add a 200ml bottle to your shopping today?"

"Okay," said Rosa. "I'll take the syrup."

She saw a bottle of syrup fly into her trolley.

"Would you like to see a shelf of similar 'also bought' products, to match your shopping today?" said the woman.

Rosa looked around her. There was no queue. She wasn't holding anyone up. The till was hers alone.

"Okay, yes."

"Thank you," the woman said. "You may be interested that we have a special offer on tomato ketchup today. Many of our customers buy tomato ketchup when they have cod and potatoes in their shopping trolley."

Rosa turned, and before her stood a single stack of shelves. At each level, there were goods that, fair enough, seemed to complement a lot of what Rosa would normally buy. Peanut butter, to go with the breads. Toilet freshener to go with the loo paper. Paracetamol to go with the cough syrup. And yes, she needed the ketchup for tea with Sam.

She selected four or five goods.

"The blue screen appeared, with Stuart's voice. We have

a special for you on peanut butter today. Would you like to another jar of smooth peanut butter, at a 10% discount?"

This was getting ridiculous.

Rosa swiped no. Enough for today.

She swiped the checkout sign.

A green box appeared before her.

The woman was back.

"Are you ready to pay?" she said.

"Yes, please."

"That's great. Avalon Supermarket is running a fundraising campaign to support the charity Abandoned Animals, which helps to fund veterinary care, tracking chips, and finding new homes for cats, dogs, and other abandoned pets. Would you like to make any of the following donations to our campaign? Remember, it's entirely your choice."

A blue square appeared before Rosa.

"One pound.

"Five pounds.

"Ten pounds.

"Please speak an amount."

Rosa considered. She thought of the pile of shopping. She thought of the Tiger she'd driven to get to the supermarket.

"One pound," she said quietly, looking around again.

"I'm sorry, I didn't get that," the woman said. "Could you please try again?"

"Five," she said. "Five pounds."

"Thank you. Five pounds. Your money will go directly to

this life altering charity. That's very generous of you," said the woman. "Are you ready to pay?"

"Yes, please," Rosa said.

Finally, she thought.

"That's great. We're signing you up to Avalon Extra, which will enable free delivery to your home at a time chosen by you, after 3 p.m. today. You will also receive special offers, bonus points on all your future shops with us, and priority invitations to launch events for our stores and new branded goods. Please swipe right to go ahead."

Then in smaller writing, beneath the choice on the box in front of her: 'If you would rather wait for your goods to be collected, and boxed, ready to place in your car today, please swipe left.'

She swiped left.

"Thank you," the woman said. "Your goods will be ready in approximately 20 minutes. If you would prefer to choose Avalon Extra, free delivery and a now a bonus of five percent off all of your shopping today, please swipe right."

Twenty minutes, Rosa thought. Did she have enough time to wait?

She swiped right.

"Thank you, Mrs Bodran. Do we have permission to take payment directly from your stored bank details? Please speak clearly: Yes or No."

"Yes," she said.

"Thank you, Mrs Bodran. At what time would you like your shopping delivered to your home?"

"Five p.m.," she said.

"Thank you. We can guarantee between 5 p.m. and 5.15 p.m. We have emailed a receipt for your shopping today. Thank you for shopping with Avalon Supermarket today."

"Thank you," Rosa replied.

Rosa's vision became completely obscured by the glowing logo of Avalon Shopping Experience. She heard Stuart's voice.

"Rosa, are you happy for me to remove your headset?"

"Yes, yes," she said. "Yes, please."

8

When Stuart took the headset off, Rosa still had the glow of the logo imprinted on her retina. She rubbed her eyes and blinked, trying to get rid of it. Finally, her eyes settled.

"It takes some getting used to, doesn't it?" Stuart said.

"Yeah, it feels so real in there. Can't believe it. How long did it take?"

"Fifteen minutes in all."

"Wow, that's incredible."

He didn't react.

"Mrs Bodran, on a scale of one to ten, how much did you enjoy your shopping today, with one being not at all, and ten being very much?"

"I guess it's a seven or eight. It got a bit frustrating."

"Sorry, could you please select a number between one and ten, with one being not at all, and ten being very much?"

"Okay, let's say seven."

"Thank you. Mrs Bodran, on a scale of one to ten, how

well would you rate our range of goods on offer today, with one being not at all, and ten being very much?"

"Hold on, are we doing some kind of survey? I'm not sure I have time?"

"Mrs Bodran, thank you for your feedback. I believe you agreed to take a survey at the beginning of your Avalon Shopping Experience today. Are you happy to continue? We're happy to offer you a £5 voucher for your next shop with us, subject to a minimum £30 expenditure. It will be added to your Avalon Extra account."

"How many questions are there?"

"That will depend on your answers," said Stuart. "I can guarantee a maximum of three minutes more. And every answer will go towards improving your own personal shopping experience in the future, as well as those of fellow shoppers."

"Okay," said Rosa. "Shoot."

"Thank you. Mrs Bodran, on a scale of one to ten, how well would you rate our range of goods on offer today, with one being not at all, and ten being very much?"

And so it went on, with Rosa answering questions, which seemed to go down small rabbit holes to pin down her experiences, then back to a primary set of standard questions.

She'd not enjoyed the meat counter experience, she'd said. Stuart asked her for more detail: presentation of the butcher, selection on offer, VR experience of the product on sale, convenience of shopping.

She'd not appreciated being offered health information in the booze section, and the questions led down a labyrinth of whether health was a priority for her and her family, whether retailers and companies should have responsibility for the outcomes of the goods they sold, where government legislation and choice should stop and begin.

Big questions, with just a few moments to answer.

"One more question," Stuart said. "Do you have any further feedback to offer about your Avalon Shopping Experience today?"

Rosa considered the discomfort she'd felt about being hit up for a charity donation at the end.

Just when she was about to spend over £100 on herself, including a fairly decent whack on alcohol, she was prompted to part with pocket change for puppies with no homes.

There was an obvious manipulation there. But then again, hadn't there been throughout the shop of one kind or another?

"No, no further feedback," she said.

"That's great. Did I fulfil my promise?" said Stuart.

"Promise?"

"I guaranteed it would be cheaper and quicker than your usual shop at Mancro."

"It was certainly quicker. And yes, I guess, if I'd bought as much as I did with you there, it would have been more pricey. But I usually get my vegetables on the High Street. And my breads."

"Well, we must be cheaper than those independent stores?"

"Yes, obviously, and more convenient."

"Great then, guarantee fulfilled."

"That's not quite the point," said Rosa.

"Sorry, I'm not sure I understand," said Stuart.

"It doesn't matter," said Rosa.

"Okay, thanks so much for your time and custom today, Mrs Bodran. We hope to see you again soon."

He didn't seem to want to hang around any further. And Rosa was pleased she didn't have to stack the car with shopping in this weather.

And she was pleased she'd saved enough time to have a peek in at least one or two of the shops she'd seen on her way in.

9

First was the travel agency.

The lovely picture of Valencia in the window was still there, the sun going down over the Roman Bridge. In another picture, a family sat in the shadows, overlooking a perfect beach. They were sharing a meal. The kids, obviously enjoying fish with cubed potatoes. The adults, a spicy chorizo perhaps, with fresh salad. Between them was placed a bottle of deep red Rioja, exactly the brand Rosa had swiped into her trolley at the supermarket.

The price for a brief break in the south of Spain, leaving and returning during the half term school break, including all flights and transfers, appeared at the bottom of the screen.

"Family of five?" it said. "Youngest child goes free!"

The price was astoundingly low.

"Book today, and this price is guaranteed. All extra luggage space on flights included. Let us take care of you."

Rosa entered the shop. The screens before her were all presenting the same offer.

"Can I help you at all?" a young man addressed Rosa as she looked at a screen.

"No, I think I've got what I need already," she said.

She texted Sam.

Three minutes later, the trip was booked. An email confirmation was on its way. The kids would be delighted.

Rosa felt a warm glow. She couldn't wait to get home to Sam. That Rioja was going to taste so good tonight.

———

Outside the travel agents, Rosa checked her watch again.

Just one more shop, then she really would have to return to the Tiger, and the dealership. She wouldn't have a chance to try out its boot, what with the convenience of the Avalon delivery later on, but the weather at least would put it through its paces.

She enjoyed driving it too. And with time ticking, she'd have to push all the right buttons to get back to the dealership, get the kids picked up, and back in time for the Avalon delivery.

But which was it to be?

An email message flashed up on her phone.

"Freaking out with the weather? Come and see us at our new store. Show this message for 10% off."

She opened the message. It was from Freakout.

"Work out the poor weather with us. We've 10% off for in store purchases of rain gear, wet weather boots, umbrellas, gloves and scarves."

For just a moment, Rosa was shocked that she'd received the text message while she was standing right outside a Freakout store. But after this morning's experience, it didn't take her long to work out she'd received the message exactly *because* she was there.

Technology.

Was it exploiting her, or was she, with all the discounts she was getting, exploiting the shops? Either way, she was getting convenience and choice.

It's entirely my choice, she thought.

Freakout was indeed full of rain and poor weather gear. On the roof above, she could hear the rain hammering down. The howling, whipping of the wind.

She'd left her anorak in her own car at the dealership. She knew her wardrobe wasn't keeping up with what had seemed, more and more, like the rapidly changing weather patterns around the UK. It could be warm where she lived, but across the other side of London, flooding. Clear in Manchester, practically snowing in Liverpool.

Talking about appalling weather was no longer a British pastime. It felt mandatory. It had become a habit for Rosa to pack wet and dry weather wear for the kids and Sam, when they went out for the day.

She looked down at her shoes and felt a little damp in her toes from running across the carpark to Avalon half an hour ago. Flat pumps had seemed like a good idea for test driving, but were hardly good rainwear. She tried on a pair of sturdier shoes. Not quite walking boots, but certainly weatherproof. The style was the familiar slightly punky brand she liked about Freakout, and the boots felt like a perfect fit.

"Can I help you, Mrs Bodran?"

"Well, yes. I guess, I've helped myself," she said. "Is it okay if I take these boots? Buy them, then wear them out to the carpark?"

"Of course," said a young man, wearing a Freakout t-shirt with the same funky branding as the boots. "A lot of our customers like to take some extra waterproofing spray for those kinds of shoes. Judging by today, it might be something you want to consider?"

"No, just the boots, thanks," said Rosa, smiling and laughing to herself. Upselling again?

"No problem," he said. "I'll put a note on your account here, so you can get some half price next time you shop with us."

"Half price?" she said. "Online?"

"No, just in the shop, Mrs Bodran. But your purchase of the boots will still earn you Freakout credits on your account."

"Go on, I'll have the spray," she said. "Half price, yes?"

"Half price, and I'll give you an extra credit on your account to say thanks."

Rosa paid for the boots, and the man gave her a branded Freakout plastic bag to carry her damp flat shoes out of the shop.

Mug, she said to herself as she approached the doors. Then she spied the puddles on the road she'd have to skip through to get to the Tiger.

She pulled her sweater up around her neck, and braced herself for the downpour. Just outside the auto opening doors, underneath a small canopy, a man was sitting in ragged clothes. A small paper cup placed before him.

She looked down, patted her jeans pockets, felt only her purse. No coins, no cash. Only swipeable cards, her phone packed with coffee reward apps, and a picture of Sam and the three kids.

"Sorry," she mumbled, as she passed the man, stepped from under the shelter and into the rain.

10

The rain came down in sheets, and when Rosa reached the car, she was beginning to feel it soaking through her jeans. She came to a stop at the Tiger, then felt around her pockets for the keys.

She couldn't find them. She cursed, as she looked in her handbag, then in the plastic Freakout bag. Maybe she'd locked the key in the car.

She tried the handle. It opened easily. She dived into the Tiger and pulled the door closed. Sitting in the driver's seat created an uncomfortable lump on her backside, at the very bottom of her jeans pocket.

There, of course, was the key fob. It had auto unlocked the door, and even as she was pushing her butt up and awkwardly trying to reach in the pocket of wet jeans, she felt warmth blowing into the car through its air conditioning system.

She put the key fob down in a pocket in the car door, threw the bag of old shoes into the passenger footwell, pulled on her safety belt, and pressed the ignition.

Immediately the windscreen wipers went into overdrive,

and the all the windows began to de-steam from the little condensation she'd brought into the cabin.

The Tiger purred beneath her, and she checked the mirrors. Despite the wipers back and front running quickly, she felt she couldn't get a decent enough view through the rain to reverse safely out of the parking spot.

She could have waited for the rain to pass. But it didn't look like that was going to happen soon. She needed to rush, but she didn't have car seats for the kids in the Tiger. There was no choice. She had to go back to the dealership first.

She put on her flashers to give the car extra visibility and put the car into reverse. The screen on the dashboard lit up and immediately gave her a clearer view from all points around the car. She was still hesitant, constantly checking her mirrors, not quite releasing herself to the technology.

The auto reverse button flashed on the screen.

Trust me.

Rosa felt a little desperate. Would she really allow the Tiger to take over? The kids weren't on board. She'd give it a go.

She pressed the button. Smoothly, but quicker than she expected, the Tiger backed itself out of the tight parking space. It stopped and sat, engine still purring, as if it wanted to be stroked.

Now Rosa had a clearer view, she had the confidence to turn off the flashers and drive the car forward and out of the carpark.

———

Time was still ticking, but if anything was going to hold her up, it wouldn't be the car. It seemed built for these poor conditions.

It was the traffic.

Other cars and vans, most of which didn't have the thicker tyres, the raised chassis, the responsive tech, and the purring audacity of the crimson beauty she was travelling in.

She sat in traffic to get out of the shopping centre. Then she sat in traffic to get to the first set of traffic lights. She located the dealership on the screen. The Tiger estimated it would be ten minutes, but could be 20 depending on the weather.

Rosa cursed the cars in front. And her own car, she couldn't quite remember the make and model, parked at the dealership. Once she'd dropped the Tiger off, she'd be in the same boat as the rest of them. Struggling to see through windscreens, slowing down for puddles, hesitating at crossings.

The weather was really setting in. If things didn't improve, and improve quickly, she might well be late for the twins after all. Maybe even for Matthew. His teachers at the school gave her the most grief when she was late, which was often. Particularly when the weather was bad, and teachers were in their own rush to join the slow moving half drowned rats queueing up at every junction, in a slow slog to get home.

And if she'd have to spend time at her eldest's school, explaining and apologising, she'd be late for the Avalon delivery. Rosa wondered who to call first: the dealership, the twin's school, Matthew's teacher or Avalon to postpone.

The lights changed, and Rosa missed her chance to search for any of the numbers. The sight and sound of the rain prevented her from confidently calling out to the onboard screen to find and dial the numbers she needed.

Instead, she tried to concentrate on the traffic around her as it continually sped up, quickly slowed, stopped, then sped up again. She knew the way to the dealership from here, but couldn't do anything to stop lights flashing, horns blaring, disgruntled drivers waving their hands as others squeezed in their vehicles where they didn't belong.

She was going to be late, that was for certain. Eventually, she felt she could face the traffic no more.

"Tiger!" she shouted.

"Yes, Mrs Bodran, what can I do for you?"

"Can you find an alternative route to the dealership?"

"Sure," said the inbuilt computer. "Taking the weather into account, I can direct you there in fifteen minutes. Are you happy to proceed?"

Rosa couldn't imagine how, given the rain and the traffic. It was hailing fiercely now, and cars were pulling over at the side of the road, flashers on, their drivers no longer feeling safe enough to continue.

"Yes," Rosa said.

"Go left at the next turning," the Tiger said. "Then proceed for half a mile."

Rosa did as she was told and was quickly on a housing estate. All the cars were going the other way; towards where the traffic had been. Each of the drivers seemed frustrated, and stared at her in the large vehicle, as it went the opposite direction.

Following the instructions, Rosa made several turns down back roads, the Tiger swinging comfortably around them. It came to an unpaved track, where Rosa came to a stop.

"Go forward for one hundred metres, then turn right," the Tiger said.

"Are you sure?"

"Go forward for one hundred metres, then turn right," it repeated.

"Okay."

Rosa drove down the track, feeling the vehicle rocking as it hit potholes and slight rises in the banks at each side. At a farm, she turned right, and was back on paved road again. She sped up, and could see over a small hill, the civilisation she had momentarily left behind. Houses surrounded both sides of the road, but as she approached the end, she realised why most would never have taken this route.

There were solid steel barriers on each side at the end, leaving a very narrow gap between them. There was a speed bump in the middle. Each of the barriers showed dents, scrapes, scratches, and colours where paint had come off car doors.

In normal weather, Rosa may just have attempted it in her own car. In this monster, in the blizzard of a hailstorm, no way.

"Nice try," she said to the screen. "There's no way we're getting through there. And I'm not paying for any damages."

She put the car into reverse and backed up. She'd have to reverse into someone's driveway, then head back down the track. As reliable and rough as the Tiger was, she realised it didn't have the capability to nip through gaps like smaller cars.

I guess that's what test drives are all about. The Tiger had failed.

11

She was about to touch the screen, to get the number for the twin's school, when the dashboard on the Tiger spoke:

"Go forward for one hundred metres, then turn left onto the main road. The dealership is on your right after thirty metres."

"I can't," Rosa said aloud, reversing.

"Go forward for one hundred and ten metres, then turn left onto the main road. The dealership is on your right after thirty metres."

"You stupid thing," she said.

"Go forward for one hundred and twenty metres, then turn left onto the main road. The dealership is on your right after thirty metres."

She stopped the vehicle, intending to turn off the GPS instructions. She could just about make her way out of here, and back down the track, if it didn't keep bleating at her.

"Would you like to go into autopilot?" said the Tiger before her fingers touched the screen.

"Repeat, please?" she said.

"Would you like to go into autopilot?"

She considered the offer.

"Estimated time to destination," she said.

"Two minutes to the dealership in the current weather and traffic conditions," the Tiger said.

"Alternative routes?"

"Fifteen minutes to the dealership in the current weather and traffic conditions."

Ah, stuff it.

If the Tiger got a scratch, or even stuck between those posts, she could blame the technology. She didn't remember giving the dealership her credit card details, anyway. There was no way they could charge her for the damage.

"Would you like to go into autopilot?"

Rosa swiped right for yes, and said, "take it away" out loud.

The screen turned to red, with a stop sign covering most of the interactive window.

"Entering autopilot," the Tiger said.

Suddenly, the vehicle was on the move. And not slowly. Rosa would have crept between those two barriers, but the Tiger only seemed to increase in speed as it approached them.

She held her breath, pulled tight on the seatbelt, and grabbed the steering wheel, which was now fixed in place.

The Tiger cleared the barriers without a grunt or a scratch. Rosa gasped for breath as it powered through at least 20 miles per hour, if not quicker. The car continued a few tens of metres down the road, towards a T-junction, where it came to a stop.

Rosa reached out and pressed the screen to stop the autopilot feature.

"Autopilot disengaged," the Tiger said.

"Wow," she said. "That was," she was going to say 'amazing'. But she was totally freaked out... "crazy."

Rosa struggled again to see through the windows, to check whether there were cars coming, or whether she was clear to pull out onto the main road. But there was no way she was going to try her luck with the autopilot again.

She waited until she saw the consistent flashing of headlights, a kind gesture from another driver she presumed, for her to proceed. She slowly pulled out into the traffic, drove one minute down the road, and pulled into the dealership.

Underneath its covered forecourt, she took a deep breath. She was definitely late, but not as late as she might have been. There wouldn't be time to chat with Kieran, but he was bound to follow up with her later.

She left the car, grabbed her bags, and quickly approached the dealership office. She entered the building and rang a bell at the empty desk there. No-one appeared.

After all the rushing, no one was there for her to give the key fob to. So she could quickly get back on the road.

She rang again and knocked hard on the countertop. Still no-one. She waited for a few minutes, so she could call school, and then she'd just leave the key on the desk and go find her own car herself. She took a seat to wait, pulling out her phone to find the numbers she needed.

It was only then she realised the headache she'd started the day with had crept back again into her right temple.

It had been there all day. A distance heavy feeling in her

stomach too. The traffic, the stress, the weather. She couldn't even remember the last time she'd eaten, but she didn't quite fancy it.

It was then that Rosa passed out.

12

On the Spaceship Renewal, the People's Museum of World History spread across a corner of the fourth level, making up about an eighth of the People's Free Expression Area of the vessel.

In one of twenty isolated booths, a young woman called Rosa Bodran was having a thin electronic probe removed from her right temple.

A gentle voice coaxed the woman out of her sleep, while a man affixed a small paper stitch over where the incision had been made and a little blood was now leaking.

"Rosa," the woman said. "You can come back to us now."

Rosa's mind was hazy, her head hurt a little. But not as much as it had been. She blinked, and eventually made out dimmed lights above, and understood that she was seated in a comfortable chair. Two shadows were moving around in her peripheral vision.

"Rosa, can you confirm your passenger number please?" the man said.

Rosa scrunched her eyes, reached into her mind.

"Seven nine eight six four," she said, surprising herself.

"That's great," said the woman. "Thanks for being part of our voluntary trial. We hope we'll get far more volunteers to help steer Control in the right direction.

"For New Earth's sake," said the man.

The two both seemed mildly familiar.

"Rosa, how did you find the experience?" said the woman.

"Uncomfortable," she said. "I mean, I'm used to VR. But this was so real, and, well, you know..."

"Yes, we've all had the same experience."

"I'm pretty nervous now," Rosa said.

"You needn't be," said the man. He seemed to be in charge. "And if you don't want to go through the personal data awareness process, you don't have to. We have the data we need."

"No," said Rosa. "No, definitely. I need to know. It's my duty to know."

"Good for you," said the woman. "So, your relaxation booth is ready, and we should have your results in about fifteen minutes."

"If only upstairs felt the same way," said the man.

The pair helped Rosa up from the easy chair. She was a little unsteady on her feet.

"It helps to look at the horizon, to get your natural balance back," she said.

"I'm okay." Rosa said. She moved slowly at first, then more confidently, following the sign back to the booth where she remembered she'd left her rucksack and comms unit.

There were freshly made smoothies, as well as protein snacks, laid out on a table by the booths, and she took a fruit flavoured drink and an oat based biscuit.

To be honest, she just wanted to sleep. But she felt it

important to obey the instructions posted on the wall of her booth. She'd committed to volunteering, after all.

She closed the door, sat and swiped the screen.

Thank you for participating in the People's Museum of World History: Learning for a Better Future project. The journey you have just been on will help all our communities to create a better future for all of us. Please sit back and relax. If you have chosen to learn your personal results, they should be ready in just 15 minutes.

Rosa took a bite of the oat biscuit and drank the smoothy from the solid starch cup. She watched pictures of the vessel she was riding in appear on the screen as the video continued.

The Spaceship Renewal is the biggest vessel ever constructed by humankind, and as a passenger, you have been given the opportunity to forge a better future for us all.

The picture cut to videos of hurricanes and flooding.

The early 2020s were a wakeup call for Planet Earth. The long predicted climate crisis affected all communities the world over. Instead of improving, the developing world became a place of hunger, flooding, abnormal weather patterns, war, and increased desperate migration.

By 2030, the world had split into two halves. Barriers were erected to control migration from hot, flooding, and weather beaten areas of the globe. But those on the richer side of the barriers suffered seriously too.

Governments had failed to act on climate change, and as predicted by scientists, a now unstoppable cycle of heat, critical weather, flooding, poverty, and war ensued.

At the World Climate Change Summit of 2036, world leaders decided that the fight to save Planet Earth had been lost. Rapid plans were drawn up to create a vast vehicle to take people away from Planet Earth, in an attempt to create and build a new, more sustainable environment at New Earth, a planet newly discovered in 2034.

The Spaceship Renewal was launched successfully in 2039, with a capacity of 100,000 new settlers. Passengers were elected to join the mission, by world leaders, by the scientific establishment, from religious bodies, and the remaining 25 percent from a lottery among those who were able to vote.

The Spaceship Renewal is predicted to land on New Earth in 2056, ship-travel time.

The People's Museum of World History, Learning for a Better Future project is an independent research programme, completely separate from Control, the panel charged with governing Spaceship Renewal and planning the settlement of New Earth.

We are carrying out independent research about how human behaviour may have contributed to the catastrophe that erupted on Planet Earth. We hope Control will listen to and act on the conclusions and suggestions of this project.

Thank you once again for your participation.

The video finished, and Rosa stared at the glowing logo of the Museum.

It hadn't taught her anything she didn't already know. She regarded it as just one of many campaign videos she'd seen.

She knew the 'Museum' was just one of many societies, non-governmental bodies, and think tanks on board. Each with their own ideas and strong opinions on New Earth and how it should be run.

The Museum's approach, she felt, was pretty neutral. It aimed to be science based, an ongoing project to harvest data, in order to model what went wrong.

But there were statistics, and models, and arguments, and positions back then on Planet Earth. None of them had prevented what happened. Why should they now?

She'd volunteered because she really wanted to know for herself what impact she and others like her might have had. The project was as good as any other on the ship, and her inclination was to trust science first.

Rosa had chosen to visit the year 2025 in the Museum's VR module. She would only have been 12 back then. But she wanted to go back in time to experience 2025 as an adult. She'd chosen an experience which would make her feel, and act, like a woman of 38.

She was intrigued about what it had felt like, back then, to live the life of a woman with children. The rest, she told the Museum, was up to them.

13

———

Rosa was guided through to a large, comfortable office, with easy chairs, a selection of drinks, and a big flat screen.

"I'm Doctor Nimit Anya, I'm a psychoanalyst and statistician on the team here at the Museum," said the man who had fixed her plaster earlier. He was standing, offering his hand to Rosa.

"You've already met my colleague, volunteer Zofia Sloane?"

Rosa nodded, and the woman smiled kindly. They all took a seat.

"Mrs Bodran, I need to be clear that you consent to being shown your personal data from our study, and that you understand that whatever you come to learn here, is conjecture only. This is a learning process, for the good of New Earth, not something to look back on with either pride or regret. Do you understand that?"

"Yes Doctor, I understand."

He smiled. "You need to remember; this was a simulation. The VR experience isn't perfect, so there's always going to be a margin of uncertainty. Plus, you chose a module that looked back to when choices and society were very different."

"Yes, Doctor."

"And finally, we're working for a better New Earth, not looking back with regret at the one we had to leave behind."

"Yes, Doctor, I understand."

"Okay, formalities over."

The doctor sighed and sat back in his chair. His whole demeanour suddenly became more relaxed.

"Sorry, we have to go through that. Personal protection and consent. All the usual stuff."

"He's a stickler for the rules," said Sloane.

"Indeed. I used to work for Control, before becoming freelance. This time, *really* independent. Rather than being told what to say. I've seen many thousands of volunteers, so there's nothing that won't surprise me. You're in safe hands."

"Oh, thank you, I feel less nervous."

"Good, let's get on with it."

"Rosa Bodran, you are passenger number 79,864. We're so glad you could join our research. Let's have a look, shall we?"

14

———

"Well, we put you in our shopping trip simulation," said Doctor Anya. "The Avalon Shopping Experience. How did you find it?"

"A bit unnerving, I suppose. Fun, but, well, it got repetitive."

"Let's look at the choices you made. You got the terrible weather simulation, bad luck there," said Sloane.

On the screen played a visualisation of a blank figure at a car dealership. In the background, the weather was getting dim.

"That's me?" asked Rosa.

"Yes. You won't see a full rendering of your own body. We don't have the budget for that. So, you picked the Tiger, and I like the colour you chose," said the doctor.

"Was that okay?"

"Well, you selected the diesel version, rather than electric. But I'm not here to judge. And remember, it's all a simulation."

His colleague, Sloane, spoke up: "You need to understand, Rosa, these were choices between what the programme generated for you. As you'll see, there is a big question about *choice* as a concept in a trial like this."

"So," continued the doctor. "Large capacity rear end, room for three children. Rugged wheels. A beast of a car."

"I chose the child option, but didn't expect there to be twins. I ended up with three!" said Rosa, almost feeling she had to defend herself.

"Aha, one unpredictable," said Anya. "It changes things, doesn't it? All the choices you make with toddler twins are completely different from if you were single, or a couple, or just had one child."

"Like I say," said Sloane. "We'll explore what really are choices a little later on."

The doctor continued, a little impatiently it seemed: "You made the choice to go to Avalon Supermarket Experience, though to be honest, with the weather as it was - and it really was like that in London in 2025, pretty consistently - you were bound to go there. Rather than to what you thought was your normal shopping centre.

"And the High Street shopping, the bakers, the fruit man, they were all quickly off the agenda given the weather we gave you."

"I'm sorry," said Rosa.

"Not at all. Not your fault. Same choice as many of our participants, placed in the same module. You were reacting to the situation you found yourself in. That's what's most interesting about this study."

"How did you find Avalon?" asked Sloane.

"Totally spooky, at least at the beginning. I don't understand that."

"What do you mean?" she asked

"Well, it's not like I'm not used to VR."

"Yes, but your experience was back in 2025," said Sloane.

"VR was only just coming into use, and only one or two retailers were making the most of it. It was programmed to be an unfamiliar experience for you."

"Okay," said Doctor Anya, "let's not linger. Let's look at the choices."

The video moved to inside the supermarket, and the shadow of Rosa shopping.

"The VR offered to better any shopping experience you'd had before - hard to refuse - and that Stuart is quite charming. Within minutes, you'd piled in your usual shop, without much of a second thought?"

"Yes," said Rosa, shaking her head.

"So, we're talking all the packaging, the cardboard, the plastics, the glass, the convenience food. With only minor consideration?"

"Yes, I swiped it all in because it was quicker," said Rosa, frowning a little with embarrassment.

"And then there was the buy the third for half price offers, the other temptations?"

"I have no willpower."

"No," said Sloane. "The VR version of you had limited will, given the choices presented to you: lack of time, the need to pick up the kids, the weather."

"Let's visit the ethical choices module," said the doctor.

"Oh, gosh, I'm embarrassed," said Rosa.

"Not at all, in fact you're engaging with the ethical module actually reduces your impact on Planet Earth, whatever the choices you made afterwards. Studies have shown that those who engage in discussion and debate over, for example, food choices or sourcing produce, are more likely to make lower impact choices overall.

"So the system credits you for engaging, and you lose only a little for some choices you actually made as a result," said Anya. "Let me see: olive oil, fish and meat?"

"Yes, then I switched it off," said Rosa.

"Of course you did," said the doctor. "Life was frustrating back then, with this campaign group, or that charity, or the other government body telling us what we should and shouldn't be doing."

Sloane spoke up: "Part of our research is about whether that constant barrage of judgement, the shaming, if you like, actually made things worse. Did people just switch off making the best choices, because they were tired of being battered by conflicting opinions, and many so called 'ethical choices' contradicted each other? This is a message we're trying to get to Control."

"So, do I get credit for switching it off?"

"Our survey of nearly 80,000 participants has modelled that your behaviour was completely natural, given the circumstances. But you don't get credit for doing it. Choosing to reject the offer to be ethical is not the same as making solid ethical choices or choosing to make unethical choices."

"It's a minefield," said Rosa.

"Yes, it's strange how what ought to have been a simple shopping trip turned out to have so many layers, when looking back. But our volunteers have been pretty consistent. It makes for good data," said the doctor.

"Shall we move onto the fruit and vegetables?" he continued.

"If we must." Rosa shook her head, but she felt she was taking the results in good spirit.

"Okay, so we abandoned the High Street option. The 5 a.m. guy, who drove to London every day, to bring back fresh produce, charged you more, but provided a good, friendly service?"

"Oh, no!" said Rosa.

"Well, first, let's look at his carbon footprint - driving to London in a big diesel van every day. Collecting a van's worth of stuff only, not big bulk, and bringing it back. Repeat daily, for six days a week. Then there's the heating, cold storage, minor packaging, and poor efficiency of a small space for retail to account for.

"Now compare that with one colossal beast of a lorry, bringing a few tonnes of produce in one trip, direct from suppliers to one place, to be taken away directly by customers. You would have had to drive to his store, as well as to the supermarket, adding an extra journey.

"In terms of carbon footprint there, it's not quite clear which method is more efficient transport wise. So, we have to look also at packaging instead."

Sloane spoke up: "When we rushed you in the VR simulation, you began swiping fruit and vegetables into your trolley, without too much consideration."

On the screen, the shadow of a figure could be seen down the fruit and veg aisle. The way it swiped produce into the trolley was almost like a cartoon. Rosa smiled, but shook her head.

"So, packaging concerns went out the window, in favour of convenience. Am I right?" said the doctor.

"I couldn't delay picking up the kids, and the weather was so rubbish."

"A very fair choice, a good trade off perhaps?" said Sloane.

Rosa spoke up: "I think if I'd have spent more time, I'd have made better choices. Loose produce, rather than packaged. I guess, inconvenienced myself?"

"But did you really have a choice?" asked Sloane.

"Shall we visit the alcohol aisle?" said Doctor Anya.

Again Rosa smiled. "Now, I really had the wool pulled over my eyes there."

"That's just what supermarkets were doing back then. They'd learned from the online shops. Offers too good to refuse, and suddenly you have way more than you'd come in for."

"So, an ethical punishment for me?"

"We don't use words like that. Our modelling showed your alcohol purchase was about normal actually. And not a significant contributor to pressure on worldwide health services, nor to natural resources. Pretty much neutral. Back then it was known that high amounts of alcohol consumption caused significant and chronic conditions, and governments and others tried to counteract that. But we all loved a drink."

"I was 12 in 2025."

"Yes, but remember, we programmed you to be 38 years old. You had three kids, no time, lots of stress, and a glass of wine was a fair release for you. I think you can be excused. Even for the vodka. Your alcohol shop was below average."

"So, now we get to the checkout," said Sloane.

"Oh, gosh," said Rosa, pushing her face into her hands.

15

"This is a classic trick the web stores perfected before the supermarkets really got into it. But I think it was that old burger chain McDonalds that started the trend.

"Have you ever heard the phrase 'would you like fries with that?'"

"Yeah, it's an urban tale?" said Rosa.

"Well, it *was* a real thing until about 2030 when it was banned," said Doctor Anya.

"The staff at pretty much every burger joint were trained to ask it, just casually, every time someone ordered a burger or even a milkshake. One in three times, customers would say yes, without considering how much it added to their bill. They wanted the fries, it didn't occur to them to look up the price. They got the fries, and the burger bars made an extra sale every three times they asked. More sales, more packaging, more waste, more natural resources wasted."

"I remember my dad would always come back with more food than we needed," said Sloane.

The doctor continued: "Once the big tech companies got a taste of that, it became an industry. How to up-sell for those extra few dollars or pounds, costing them very little or nothing, but boosting their profits. After all, you were already at the shop, you'd already got most of your shopping, the rain was pouring, it was no extra effort for you to slip a few extra things into the trolley.

"First online bookshops, then the supermarkets. Then, with VR supermarket experiences too," said the doctor.

"You didn't even have to make choices," said Sloane. "The algorithm had noticed the combination of fish and chips, often bought with ketchup. It was obvious you would take it."

"It was convenient," said Sloane. "Convenient for us all, and super convenient for the shops to shift more goods. Everyone wins."

"Well, hardly," said Rosa. She considered the spaceship she was in now. Hadn't they destroyed the Planet Earth with all that packaging and convenience?

"Did everyone win?" she said.

Doctor Anya shook her head. Rose saw a look to Sloane - time to move on.

"Let's quickly go over the next part, as this is what many feel most uncomfortable with," said Sloane

"No, I know what's coming," said Rosa. "I asked for a full analysis. And it's really important for me to know. I want to be really clear, on New Earth, what I can do better."

The doctor hurried things along: "So, after you put five extra goods into your trolley, that you didn't think of before they were suggested to you..."

"Go on," said Rosa, staring at the ground.

"You were asked if you'd like to make a charitable donation?"

"Yes, and I donated five pounds to Abandoned Animals."

"That's right. Why did you select that amount?"

Rosa was silent.

"It's okay," said Sloane. "It's part of the survey."

"Well, I wanted to give £1, as I don't enjoy having my arm twisted that way. But, well, I was embarrassed to be giving so little."

"Did you notice anything about the choice of donations?"

"What, other than you couldn't choose to give nothing?" said Rosa.

"Well, you could have done, but that would have been to select *Other*, and then to declare you would not make a donation."

"Go on," said Rosa.

"Well, shopping for goods at Avalon was as easy as swiping this way and that. Swipe a treat for yourself, and in it went to your trolley.

"But at Avalon, it forced you to speak out loud the donation you would give. In front of another person."

"Oh, you tricked me."

"The power of subconscious influence, that's all," said the doctor. "You were forced to give to a charity we already knew you wouldn't be particularly interested in. Remember, the Rescue Children shop right outside the door? And later, when you honestly wanted to give some money to the homeless man, you had no means to do so."

"The smartest, richest, most manipulative techniques work," said Sloane. "Those without the resources to pull those tricks - or more likely engage with companies that did it for them - lost money, time after time.

"Even the charity sector became unbalanced. The richer charities became richer, the poorer ones struggled. They had no power to raise awareness of the humanitarian disasters that were threatening to take place, and that eventually brought Planet Earth to its knees," added the doctor.

"Homelessness was rife. But at least those poor little puppies had safe, warm, middle class homes to go to."

"Shall we move onto the checkout?" said Sloane quickly.

"Avalon Extra?" Rosa smacked her head. "You totally reeled me in there."

"Well, once again," said Sloane, "you weren't given much of a choice. Either wait twenty more minutes for your shopping, or have it delivered for free. Not much of an option, with it now hailing outside? And the system detected, since you were so keen on the half price goods and the discounts, that's exactly how Avalon Extra would be up-sold to you."

"These things were tested to their very limits, in the early 2020s," said the doctor. "So much so that every interaction you would have had with, say, an online store, was tailored to be slightly different. From the tint of the logo, to the colour of the Buy Now button, to the layout of the shop.

"Millions of tiny adjustments, made over millions of purchases by millions of people, to create the online shop that would persuade you - Mrs Rosa Bodran - and you alone, that your shopping experience was enjoyable, quicker, easier, and that everything you were buying was something you wanted, needed or would allow yourself as a treat.

"Every single person's shopping experience was ever so slightly different, perfectly tailored to them, but so subtle it wasn't worth mentioning to anyone else, if we noticed at all."

"And once Avalon Extra *had* you," said Sloane, "you were always more likely to shop there in the future. Because now you had your monthly fee to pay, but all those lovely discounts specially designed for you."

It was the doctor's turn to speak: "It's why the High Streets eventually couldn't survive, despite the goodwill of people exactly like you. The offer was just too good to refuse, particularly as the climate, the traffic, and the world around you made it so difficult to do anything else."

"God, I feel so awful," said Rosa. "Like manipulated, but also, well, I should have been stronger. If only all of us had been stronger, then this all," she indicated the ship around her, "it never might have happened."

"It's okay," said Sloane. "Everyone was to blame, but also not to blame. That's what we've discovered here at the Museum."

"There are just two sections to go, if you're happy to proceed," said the doctor.

"It's entirely my choice," laughed Rosa. "Go on, might as well get on with it."

———

"Flights," said the doctor.

Rosa shook her head.

"According to the VR experience, you considered, booked and paid for flights in the south of Spain, in less than ten minutes. During the shopping experience, we assume, you weren't considering a holiday?"

"No," said Rosa. "I was busy buying more than I needed."

"So, you saw the too good to be true offer at the travel agents, went directly in, refused any help from the member of staff there, and booked up a return flight for five people, including transfers."

"I'm sorry," Rosa said.

"Nothing to be sorry for," said Sloane. "Flights were, of course, the key source of CO_2 emissions back on Planet Earth, 1.6 tonnes of CO_2 emission per flight, on average.

"That's only next to gases emitted by livestock. And remember, you didn't buy the extra meat at Avalon Supermarket, except what was already in your trolley. You opted for fish. A more ethical choice, at least as far as climate change is concerned. But those flights would have to create a significant total emission of CO_2."

"Given how cheap they were," said the doctor, "on some scales, the £1 you spent per ton of CO_2 emission was really quite high. But there's a mitigation, and it gets right to the heart of what is emerging from our research."

"Go on," said Rosa.

"You had a family. We had programmed your VR experience, to make you believe you were in the habit of one or two holidays abroad every year. That's why you were considering the Tiger - so you could drive to France or Spain. In fact, flying would be very rare for you."

"That's right," said Rosa. "The flight was part of the holiday. Something exciting for the kids."

"Your twins," said Doctor Anya. "They would never have been on an airplane before. You wanted to give them that experience. You weren't one of those families that flew everywhere at the drop of a hat. You and Sam didn't fly in and out to business meetings. Between you, you'd never taken a long haul flight."

"So, at £1 per ton of CO_2 emission, your impact was quite high for that single flight," said the doctor. "But your £1 for happiness, or to put it another way, your CO_2 emission measured against happiness for you and your family on a unique holiday together, well that would go a long way towards mitigating the impact of that flight."

"What the doctor means," said Sloane, "is that from taking that flight, and having that holiday in Valencia, your family would most likely have enjoyed yourself more than the alternative.

"Consider the sadness, boredom, frequent car journeys in that big Tiger vehicle to keep the kids happy, junk food, screen time, electricity and other power use. If you had *not* taken that holiday, all that would not have been equal to your CO_2 emissions. But on many other indexes, would have contributed to the factors that may have led to the Planet Earth catastrophe."

"So, one holiday was okay?" said Rosa.

"Not okay, in terms of CO_2 emissions and climate change," said the doctor. "But way better than taking lots of holidays without thinking, taking the entire family with you, time after time, to faraway places. Like I said, your impact would have been quite low compared with other families."

"That's a relief," said Rosa.

"Well, we're not quite finished yet," said the doctor. "But let's take a break before we carry on."

16

———————

Rosa sat in the clinic office, exhausted. Her mind felt busted from trying to unravel what, to begin with, had appeared to be a simple offer to be part of a voluntary study.

She took a sip of her oat smoothy. The grains were grown on board in the ship's vast greenhouse, fed and powered by artificial light.

She felt a little sick. She knew the decisions she'd made under VR were to some extent already programmed into her. It was more of a history lesson, she thought, than an attempt to apportion blame.

This was a museum, after all. A look back at the past. She already knew the key causes of the final abandonment of Planet Earth. You couldn't escape the ideas, which were drilled into you on every poster, in every lift, on every screen across the vessel.

But what she hadn't expected was that there might be some deeper explanation to why humankind had acted the way it had. The mantra of Spaceship Renewal was to learn from our mistakes, then use what we've learned to create a new, safer world on New Earth.

She was now understanding it was far more complicated than any simple slogan could encapsulate. If she was one of thousands to have gone through this trial, why didn't more people talk about it?

Perhaps the answer was what she was about to hear.

———

"Welcome back," said Doctor Anya, as Rosa came back into his office, and he asked to take her seat. "I can assure you; this is the last part of our analysis of your VR experience. And thank you again, very much, for your contribution to this project."

Rosa smiled.

Sloane shuffled her chair closer to Rosa's and put a sympathetic look on her face.

"So, the journey back in that Tiger," said the doctor.

"That was pretty wild," said Rosa.

"The weather was pretty mean. Impossible to drive in. And then there was the traffic."

"But the Tiger did a pretty good job, I have to admit that," said Rosa.

"And if you'd chosen to, it could have carried your shopping too. Then, if you weren't just test riding it, you would have picked up your kids, and driven home. Safe and sound, right? Despite the weather."

"That's why I chose the Tiger."

"But you didn't choose the electric version?"

"No, I was worried it might run out of juice, and I and the kids would be abandoned, in that weather particularly. And the weather was becoming pretty typical back then."

"Fair enough," said Sloane.

"And when the Tiger directed you to take an alternative route, to speed up your journey?"

"I was pretty impressed with that," said Rosa.

"So, why didn't you drive through those tight barriers?"

"Gosh, I would never have done that. I didn't trust myself. In fact, I wouldn't have trusted myself to drive with the kids in that weather at all."

"So, reluctantly, you allowed the car to do the driving for you. Self-drive."

"Yes, but only because I was in a rush. And only because I didn't have the kids on board. There was no way I would have allowed self-drive if I'd been risking their safety."

"Do you understand why we programmed that journey into this trial, Rosa?" said the doctor. She thought she heard sorrow in his voice, for the first time.

She thought deeply.

"It's because of the kids?"

"That's right," said Sloane.

"When you entered the VR programme, you decided the avatar you wanted was a woman of 38 years old, with kids, middle class, that was about the size of it."

"Okay," Rosa replied.

"The rest of your experience was under VR, and was tailored to that selected personality. So, you chose the Tiger, specifically because..."

"I wanted a car big enough to take the kids to school in, to do shopping in, and to perform in the crappy weather."

"So your priority was your children?"

"One hundred percent," said Rosa. "Though, I didn't expect to have three children. I guess that's why I'd opted for the biggest car available. Room for three child car seats, super safe."

"That's right. You opted to have children, but you didn't get a choice of how many kids you had, nor their gender, nor..."

"Stop. I get it. I didn't expect to have twins. It was a roll of the dice."

"Which is the same dice roll any of us take if we decide to have children, or if we have them without deciding. And when the kids come, in most cases, we love them, however many there are, am I right?"

"Of course."

"And we'll do everything we can to feed them, clothe them, keep them safe, do our very best for them."

"Absolutely," said Rosa.

"So, we're talking lots of shopping, particularly if we can get it cheap. And we are in a rush because of them, because we need to meet their needs. We get a big car, with lots of safety features, and we don't choose electric because we don't trust it not to let us down and strand our kids on the way to school. We book last minute holidays to keep them happy. We do everything, I mean everything, to be a great parent."

"That's only natural," said Rosa.

"Like you say. And it supports exactly the theory we've been developing, from all our VR trials."

"Can you explain that Doctor?"

"Sure. In the early 2020s, there was a revolution in the offering of vehicles. Big plans by governments, the western world over, to go electric. Charging stations were built. Electric cars were designed. Self-drive cars were researched, and launched to provide more efficiency and less traffic. Tax breaks promoted for electric and self-drive.

"But what was missing was demand. Families in particular, they didn't buy electric cars. They didn't think they were safe for their kids. They certainly weren't going to buy self-drive cars.

Self-drive actually scared them *off* walking or cycling to school, too. They didn't trust that a self-drive wouldn't go crazy, the sensors might go awry and mount a pavement or hit a kid on their bike.

"Parents stuck to what they knew. The motor industry went back to fossil fuels, and the market dropped out of electric and self-drive completely.

"Everyone said they wanted self-drive, electric cars. They knew it could slow down climate change, or prevent it completely. But they wanted them for everyone else, over there, out of danger. Not for themselves, their children, their neighbourhoods.

"People wanted kids, and would do anything to prevent them being in danger, including - ironically - the very thing that sent Planet Earth on the path it ended up on.

"Governments tried to promote cycling for kids. Walking to school. Walking to the workplace. But with the weather so rubbish, and the roads so unsafe, and polluted, what parent would dare allow their kids to go on two wheels or by walking? Especially when they could drive them in their big, fossil fuel, weatherproof and child safe cars?

"The same could be said for flights. We all *wanted* to reduce our mileage, but those holidays, those business meetings, those visits abroad, well, they had to be done. We'd keep them to a minimum, but as for actually deciding never to fly. That never happened."

The doctor said this last, as if it was nearing a conclusion. His analysis was nearly complete. Rosa nodded her head, convinced by the core argument.

Sloane shuffled her seat even closer to Rosa and reached out and took her hand.

The doctor spoke: "Rosa, according to our research, the biggest contributor to the factors that meant Planet Earth was no longer a viable home for humankind, was a very natural desire.

"It was the desire to have as many children as we wanted, and to do for them what we chose to do. It was that desire that trumped any choices we would make about the future of the world. Or for humanity.

"Whether we were, as parents, responsible for our own offspring's impact on the world, and subsequently their own children's impact, is a debatable question. Pure philosophy.

"But whatever the answer to that dilemma, our modelling shows that the generations of the 2000s and following, had a significant impact on climate change simply by their tendency to have children. And then for their children to have children, and so on.

"Rosa, if we're going to make New Earth viable, and not make the mistakes of the last fifty years, we have no choice. We have to remove the right for people to have children as they wish. We have to work out a fairer way to protect the population as a whole."

17

Volunteer Zofia Sloane led Rosa out of the clinic, and into an informal lounge room, close to the Museum entrance.

"How are you feeling," she asked.

"Well, pretty guilty, that's for sure."

"Yes, sorry. Doctor Anya can be pretty blunt. He means well, but I guess he's despairing about the direction Control is taking us with plans for settlement on New Earth."

The two took a seat, and Sloane passed Rosa a glass of re-purified water.

"I did volunteer," said Rosa. "I needed to see what I saw."

"Listen," said Sloane. "I have a few minutes before our next set of volunteers. I'd like to smooth out a few things with you. It makes everything easier to take. It's the missing piece that a statistician like Doctor Anya always forgets because he's so - well, he's so statistically minded."

Rosa took a sip of water. She felt her heart reduce its pace. It felt cool and settled her stomach a little.

"Go on," said Rosa.

"I'm just a volunteer here at the Museum, but I do believe in the organisation's aims, to try to influence Control on their policies towards a better future on New Earth.

"But the Museum's final report to Control is likely to be something that's quite hard to articulate. And certainly can't be easily shown in statistics."

"My head's already blown," said Rosa. "I just don't know what the future looks like anymore."

"Well, throughout the VR experience, the emphasis was all on your choice. Remember, Stuart at Avalon kept saying it. The staff at the counters too?"

"It became annoying," said Rosa.

"I guess the simulation emphasised that you had choices to make, so that our model could measure how we acted back in 2025 or whenever, when presented with options."

"But there were so many choices," said Rosa.

"Or," said Sloane, "there were really no choices at all. This is why you weren't to blame for the choices you made, and you shouldn't feel bad."

"But I do feel bad," said Rosa.

"Well think again: how much choice did you really have, and how much were you influenced? Aren't most of our actions pre-determined. We think we have choice, but really we're bound to act in certain ways depending on the options we're offered, and so much else besides."

Rosa thought for a moment: "If the supermarket used those tactics against us, then surely they are to blame. At least for influencing my choices?"

"That's exactly right. But we need to go further. What influenced the supermarket's choices? What influenced the choices of its management as a corporate body, but also as individuals with their own desires, their own families?

"What about the company's shareholders? What about the woman at the till, trying to up-sell to you to get a bigger bonus? What about the government, giving incentives and tax breaks?

"Was it Avalon's free will to design the shopping experience that way, or were each of those involved also influenced to go about things that way?"

Rosa sighed: "So we are all just the product of other people's choices and influences? And they too, the same?"

"That might be right," said Sloane. "Every action we take. Every decision we make. It's because of everything around us: our upbringing, our class, traditions, accidents, influences. It *should* be your choice. But the only way to truly make a choice is to understand how limited our choice really is.

"We all think we have a choice in life, but do we really? There are 100,000 people on this ship, and it's made up mainly of citizens from richer countries. Most on Planet Earth didn't even know of plans to leave, let alone were asked if they wanted to come along for the ride.

"The elite bought themselves a ticket, safe and sound. And duly elected themselves as Control. The remains of us, just a quarter of people on board, had to enter a lottery for the chance. Most people, even in the Western world, didn't even know about the lottery. So, *our* even being here was a matter of being offered a choice in the first place. Some didn't even get the choice."

Rosa and Zofia Sloane were quiet for a very long time.

"Thank you," said Rosa, finally. "There's a lot to think about there."

"Write it down," she said. "Or at least, that's what I've done. I have it stuck above my bunk bed and say it to myself every day. But, well it's entirely your choice whether or not to do that."

They both laughed.

Rosa felt like hugging the woman.

"Thanks again."

18

Rosa took her oat smoothy and went to relax on the sixth floor viewing platform. It was usually quiet at this time of day, and word was that just now the view was quite magnificent.

The platform had large open windows, with very comfortable seating looking all around the vessel. It was like a cinema, and people like Rosa were still amazed by space, even though they'd been living in it for five years.

She was one of those who could never tire of looking at the stars, gulping up the information that was provided on screens around the lounge about what star it was passing, at many thousands of miles an hour.

Three months ago, there had been a lot of fuss on the ship about the distant single dot, barely perceptible to the human eye. It was only just visible through the powerful telescopes on the viewing platforms. It was turning blue from white.

Control had declared a festival holiday. There were parties on every level of the ship. Alcohol was in abundance, dancing. Drunken romance had been in the air.

New Earth was two space-ship years away, and most on board knew they were now likely to land on it. Be part of building the new era.

Rosa had visited every day since, and sat in the same comfortable chair, just staring at the planet before her.

First, she'd watched as it had gone from white with a slight blue tinge to the sky blue she had remembered as a child when looking up from Planet Earth. Then it had turned to a deep sea blue as the Renewal had moved gradually closer.

It was barely perceptible, but the New Earth had become bigger. Now, as Rosa sat there, it was far more than the light blue pin prick they had celebrated.

She held her hand up. It was now a small, blue, pea sized worth of planet waiting for them.

Getting ever closer.

Asking: what are you going to do with me?

Today had been an emotional one for Rosa. She'd put off volunteering for the programme for three months, afraid of what she might learn.

As she looked out now on New Earth, she had a mixed feeling of hope and dread. She felt the same sickness she'd felt this morning. She rubbed her abdomen with both hands.

"Don't worry, little one," she said. "We're going to do a better job this time."

Dear Valued Reader,

Thank you for reading this book.

I hope you have been entertained, perhaps challenged and that you would like to read more of my writing.

Once you have left a review, please turn the page and get another of my near future thrillers absolutely **free.**

But before, it would make a real difference to me if you were able to please leave a **review** on your **social media**, share your **recommendation** with your friends, and please write an honest review on your **favourite book buying and review site.**

Thank you again for reading!
Gideon Burrows

ALSO BY GIDEON BURROWS

"Pacy, thrilling, suspenseful and complex to keep your attention... this is a must-read for anyone who likes intelligently-written thrillers - political, techno, or otherwise." ★ ★ ★ ★ ★

"The best of this genre I have read for a long time." ★ ★ ★ ★ ★

"A thought-provoking thriller. I'm already casting the film version in my mind." ★ ★ ★ ★ ★

It's 2030. A world of driverless electric cars, touch less screens and social media that knows what you want before you do.

When jaded journalist Curtis Soren meets the new powerful boss of the government's mysterious Ministry for Society, he uncovers a top-secret organisation that puts him and his colleagues in danger - and threatens the privacy and freedom of every citizen.

In a struggle with his own haunted past and a present he doesn't understand, Soren is forced to take on Portico, the biggest social media organisation of all.

It becomes a desperate battle to expose the truth in an online world of fake news, censorship and social users addicted to their screens.

Lose yourself in this thrilling page turner which will challenge how you think about the future, and what you might need to sacrifice to get there.

Please buy direct from the author

at www.gideon-burrows.com using the code 'ReadAndReview' to get any book half price

ACKNOWLEDGMENTS

Thanks to everyone who's contributed to the publication of Future Shop.

Particular thanks to Andy MacDonald, Kay Barrett and Iain MacFarlane for attention to detail in the proofing, and to my Alpha and Beta readers who continue to support my work and ensure it is as good as it can be.

Credit to Joanna Penn; an off-the-cuff comment from her on one of her excellent podcasts prompted me to think about the concept of virtual shopping and where it might lead.

www.ingramcontent.com/pod-product-compliance
Lightning Source LLC
Chambersburg PA
CBHW071233170626
46809CB00008BA/3034